The Tree House

Felice Arena and Phil Kettle

illustrated by
Mitch Vane

RISING ★ STARS

First published in Great Britain by
RISING STARS UK LTD 2004
76 Farnaby Road, Bromley, BR1 4BH

For information visit our website at:
www.risingstars-uk.com

British Library Cataloguing in Publication Data

A CIP record for this book is available from the British Library.

ISBN: 1-904591-69-8

First published in 2003 by
MACMILLAN EDUCATION AUSTRALIA PTY LTD
627 Chapel Street, South Yarra, Australia 3141

Associated companies and representatives throughout the world.

Copyright © Felice Arena and Phil Kettle 2003

Project Management by Limelight Press Pty Ltd
Cover and text design by Lore Foye
Illustrations by Mitch Vane

Printed and bound in Great Britain by
Mackays of Chatham plc, Chatham, Kent

Contents

Nick

Matt

CHAPTER 1

Just Another Day

Matt and Nick are outside Matt's house talking. Their latest plan is a ripper.

Matt "What we need is a place that's ours—somewhere we can hide where nobody can find us."

Nick "Yeah, like a clubhouse, where we can plan our next adventure."

Matt "You never know, it could be a good place to hide when we get attacked by aliens!"

Nick "Yep, you never know when that might happen. Have you ever seen any aliens?"

Matt "Only the two girls who live down the street. When they dress up and put on make-up they really look like aliens."

Nick "I wonder what planet they come from?"

Matt "I reckon it would have to be the planet pink. It must be a really weird planet where they all wear pink dresses with bows in their hair, and they're all infected with girl germs."

Nick "The planet pink! That's a good one."

Matt "Well I've heard girls talking and they don't talk about the same things as us so they must come from somewhere else."

Nick "What about Amy? She's like us, sort of. She can kick a football further than you can."

Matt "Yeah, but she's got two
brothers and they've shown her
how to do some of that stuff. Did
you know she plays cricket and
she's really good?"

Nick "You only reckon that she's
good 'cos she bowled you out."

Matt "Only because that was a
really lucky ball."

Nick "Yeah, lucky it bowled just your off stump and not your middle stump."

Matt "Anyway, what about a tree house? I think we should build our own."

Nick "Do you know where there's a good tree?"

Matt "Yeah, I saw one at the back of the house. Come and look."

CHAPTER 2

A Great Spot

Matt and Nick go to the field at the back of Matt's house. In the middle of the field is a huge tree. Matt doesn't say anything, he just points at the tree.

Nick "What a ripper! That's the best tree."

Matt "Nobody will find us in that tree, not even the aliens."

Nick "Yeah, while the rest of the world's being attacked, we'll be safe. Maybe we can even fight the aliens from up there."

Matt "Let's get started. We'll need some wood and nails and stuff. Where can we get all that?"

Nick "We could look in my dad's shed. He's got loads of tools. There's always a stack of other stuff there too."

Matt "And there's some old wood in my backyard."

Nick "We better not tell anyone what we're using."

Matt "Nah, or they'll know what we're building and it won't be a secret anymore."

Nick "This'll be our secret tree house and nobody will know where it is. Nobody."

Matt "Well, you go and get whatever you can find and so will I. Meet you back here."

Nick "Okay. See you."

The boys head off. Matt goes to his
house and scouts around for all the
things he thinks might help build
the tree house. He loads it all into
an old wheelbarrow.

Nick finds some tools and some planks in his dad's shed. He ties some rope around the end of one of the planks and drags it back to the big tree.

Matt "Wow, we've got stacks! I think we've got enough to build the best tree house ever."

Nick "You climb the tree and I'll pass the wood up."

Matt "Hang on, don't you think we should draw some plans first?"

Nick "No, that'll take too much time. Let's just build it as we go."

CHAPTER 3

The Builders

The boys string together a rope ladder
and attach it to the tree. Then they
throw a rope over one of the branches
and pull up the timber. Soon they
have everything up in the tree, and
after a lot of hammering and nailing,
something pretty much like a tree
house starts to appear.

Matt "This has to be the best tree house in the world."

Nick "Yeah and we're the only ones in the world who know it's here."

Matt "Now we need some tin or wooden bits for a roof so that when it's raining we can stay dry."

Nick "Yeah, and if we have a roof the aliens won't be able to see inside."

Matt "We might be able to get some from a fence."

Nick "Which fence?"

Matt "An old one no-one's using anymore."

Nick "How will we know that?"

Matt "Well, if nobody lives in the house, the fence is probably not being used."

Nick "So if we took some of the fence what would happen when somebody else moves in?"

Matt "Mmm, good point. Maybe that's not such a good idea. We might have to ask at home for some tin."

Nick "Yeah, and maybe we could get someone to help us put the roof on."

Matt "Sounds good, but we'll just have to make them promise not to tell anyone."

✳ Nick and Matt keep working away
on the tree house, making sure that
it's safe.

The next day, Nick's dad gives the
boys some tin from under the shed
and in no time, they are lifting the roof
on. Finally the tree house is finished.

Nick "I reckon this really is the best tree house I've ever seen."

Matt "Yeah, we'll be able to spend all our spare time here."

Nick "We'll just have to put a sign up at the bottom of the tree to keep out you-know-who."

CHAPTER 4

Making Plans

Nick and Matt nail a piece of wood to the bottom of the tree. On it they paint "Dangerous animals in tree. Keep away, especially girls".

Nick "We need to get a supply of food for our secret hideaway."

Matt "Yeah, lots of food in case the aliens attack and we have to stay up here for ages."

Nick "What will we use for weapons when we have to fight the aliens?"

Matt "We could go to the field and get some cowpats—they make the best bombs."

Nick "Yeah, as soon as a cowpat hits the aliens they'll turn their spaceship around and go back where they came from."

Matt "If it doesn't knock them out first. Maybe we should write to the army and tell them how good cowpat bombs are—they could probably use some."

Matt and Nick lie on the floor of
the tree house, looking down at the
ground below.

Nick "Look at all those ant holes
down there."

Matt "Bet I can spit straight into one."

Nick "Bet you can't"

Matt is just about to spit into the ant hole when they hear what sounds like an alien voice coming from below: "Hey you dangerous animals, can we come up?"

Matt "I think the aliens have arrived."

Nick "Yeah, and we haven't even got any bombs to drop on them."

Nick looks down at the two aliens
who are standing at the bottom of
the ladder. He sees they are the girl
aliens from down the street.

Nick "They look like those two aliens from the planet pink and they have a big basket with them."

Matt "It might be full of bombs."

"Let us up, you two—we've got lots of food."

Nick "Maybe we should have a
meeting with them and find out
what their plans are for the food."

Matt "You can come up but you
must give us the password *and* the
real thing."

Nick "And the password is 'food'."

Matt and Nick decide to enter into a peace treaty with the planet pink aliens. The aliens promise they will never tell anyone about the tree house and to always give the proper entry sign before they come up—and chocolate biscuits work best.

The latest update is that peace
with the aliens may only last as long
as the food does—they have already
started to talk about putting up pink
curtains!

Tree House Lingo

Nick

Matt

cowpat Cow poo still in the shape it came out in! It can be hard or soft, depending on how old it is.

rope ladder Used to get into the tree house. You can pull it up into the tree house when you are in it. This will stop those aliens from sneaking up on a secret meeting.

spyglass A small telescope used to look for aliens or girls who might be sneaking up on your tree house.

tree house A house built in a tree.

Tree House Must-dos

☞ Find a good tree.

☞ Make sure that the tree has strong branches.

☞ Try to find a tree that is well hidden.

☞ Don't tell anyone where your tree house is.

☞ Girls are not allowed unless they bring food.

☞ Keep some food in your tree house; you never know when you are going to be hungry.

☞ Keep sleeping bags and pillows in your tree house; you never know when you'll get sleepy.

☞ Always ask your parents before you take anything out of the garage to help build your tree house.

☞ Keep your spyglass in the tree house. You never know when the aliens might attack.

☞ Make sure that your tree house has a KEEP AWAY sign nailed on the tree.

BOYS RULE!

Tree House
Instant Info

Our ancestors lived in tree houses for safety from wild animals and their enemies.

Some tree houses have been built up to 30 metres above the ground.

The Swiss family Robinson lived in a tree house. So did Tarzan.

There are lots of people in the world who choose to live in tree houses.

There are building companies that build really large tree houses, sometimes from kits.

Some tree houses even have their own telephones.

BOYS RULE!
Think Tank

1 Where do you build a tree house?

2 What would you build first?

3 Are girls allowed in tree houses?

4 Could a lion climb up a tree and get into a tree house?

5 Do birds call their homes tree houses?

6 What kind of ladders are best for climbing trees?

7 Should you wear a crash helmet in your tree house?

8 Should you tell anyone where your tree house is?

Answers

8 Only tell your best mate where your tree house is.

7 Wear a helmet in your tree house, only if you think you might fall.

6 Rope ladders are the best ladders for climbing trees.

5 If you can get a bird to tell you, please tell us the answer—we'd really like to know.

4 A lion could climb into your tree house, but only if you are in Africa.

3 Girls are only allowed in your tree house if they bring food.

2 You build the floor first.

1 You build a tree house in a tree, of course.

How did you score?

- If you got 8 answers correct, then you are able to build your own tree house.

- If you got 6 answers correct, you had better get some help from your parents!

- If you got fewer than 4 answers correct, make sure you stay on the ground.

Felice → | ← Phil

Hi guys!

We have loads of fun reading and want you to, too. We both believe that being a good reader is really important and so cool.

Try out our suggestions to help you have fun as you read.

At school, why don't you use "The Tree House" as a play and you and your friends can be the actors. Set the scene for your play. What props do you need? You can pretend that you are in your tree house. Maybe you are expecting an attack from the aliens, the ones that look like girls!

So ... have you decided who is going to be Matt and who is going to be Nick? Now, with your friends, read and act out our story in front of the class.

We have a lot of fun when we go to schools and read our stories. After we finish the kids all clap really loudly. When you've finished your play your classmates will do the same. Just remember to look out of the window— there might be a talent scout from a television station watching you!

Reading at home is really important and a lot of fun as well.

Take our books home and get someone in your family to read them with you. Maybe they can take on a part in the story.

Remember, reading is a whole lot of fun.

So, as the frog in the local pond would say, Read-it!

And remember, Boys Rule!

BOYS RULE!

When We Were Kids

Felice *Phil*

Phil "What was great about your tree house when you were a kid?"

Felice "It had hot and cold water."

Phil "Gee, and what else?"

Felice "Two bedrooms and wall-to-wall carpet."

Phil "That has to have been one of the best tree houses in the world."

Felice "Yes it was, but there was one thing missing."

Phil "What?"

Felice "A tree!"

BOYS RULE!
What a Laugh!

Q What did the fence say to the house?

A I've got you surrounded.

43

BOYS RULE!

Read about the fun that boys have in these **BOYS RULE!** titles:

Gone Fishing

The Tree House

Golf Legend

Camping Out

Bike Daredevils

Water Rats

Skateboard Dudes

Tennis Ace

Basketball Buddies

Secret Agent Heroes

Wet World

Rock Star

and more ... !

BOYS RULE! books are available from most booksellers. For mail order information please call Rising Stars on 01933 443862 or visit www.risingstars-uk.com